A Robbie Reader

Hurricane Katrina, 2005

John A. Torres

Mitchell Lane
PUBLISHERS

P.O. Box 196
Hockessin, Delaware 19707
Visit us on the web: www.mitchelllane.com
Comments? email us:
mitchelllane@mitchelllane.com

Mitchell Lane PUBLISHERS

Printing   2   3   4   5   6   7   8   9

A Robbie Reader/Natural Disasters

The Ancient Mystery of Easter Island
The Bermuda Triangle
Bubonic Plague
Earthquake in Loma Prieta, California, 1989
The Fury of Hurricane Andrew, 1992
Hurricane Katrina, 2005
The Influenza Pandemic of 1918
The Johnstown, Pennsylvania, Flood, 1889
The Lost Continent of Atlantis
Mt. Vesuvius and the Destruction of Pompeii, A.D. 79
Mudslide in La Conchita, California, 2005
Tsunami Disaster in Indonesia, 2004
The Volcanic Eruption on Santorini, 1500 BC
Where Did All the Dinosaurs Go?
The Year of the Tornadoes, 1985

Library of Congress Cataloging-in-Publication Data
Torres, John Albert.
    Hurricane Katrina, 2005 / by John A. Torres.
        p. cm. — (A Robbie reader. Natural disasters)
    Includes bibliographical references and index.
    ISBN 1-58415-498-5 (library bound)
    1. Hurricane Katrina, 2005—Juvenile literature. 2. Disaster victims—Louisiana—New Orleans—Juvenile literature. 3. Disaster relief—Louisiana—New Orleans—Juvenile literature. 4. Rescue work—Louisiana—New Orleans—Juvenile literature.
I. Title. II. Series.
    HV636 2005 .U6 T67 2007
    976'.044—dc22   2006006109
ISBN-10: 1-58415-498-5   ISBN-13: 9781584154983

ABOUT THE AUTHOR: John A. Torres is an award-winning journalist covering social issues for *Florida Today*. John has also written more than 40 books for various publishers on a variety of topics, including *P. Diddy; Clay Aiken; Mia Hamm; Disaster in the Indian Ocean, Tsunami, 2004;* and *Hurricane Katrina and the Devastation of New Orleans, 2005* for Mitchell Lane Publishers. In his spare time, John likes playing sports, going to theme parks, and fishing with his children, stepchildren, and wife, Jennifer.

PHOTO CREDITS: Cover—Mark Wilson/Getty Images; pp. 1, 14—David J. Phillip, Pool/ AP Photo; p. 4—James Nielsen/AFP/Getty Images; p. 6—Sharon Beck; p. 8—Dave Einsel/ Getty Images; pp. 9, 20, 21—Mario Tama/Getty Images; pp. 10, 13—NOAA; p. 17—Eric Gay/AP Photo; p. 18—Kyle Niemi/U.S. Coast Guard via Getty Images; pp. 22, 23, 24, 27— Army Military.

PUBLISHER'S NOTE: The following story is based on the author's personal trip to New Orleans in September 2005, during which he interviewed dozens of survivors and witnessed the destruction firsthand. The story has been thoroughly researched and to the best of our knowledge represents a true story. While every possible effort has been made to ensure accuracy, the publisher will not assume liability for damages caused by inaccuracies in the data, and makes no warranty on the accuracy of the information contained herein.

TABLE OF CONTENTS

Words in **bold** type can be found in the glossary.

City streets became flooded after Hurricane Katrina made landfall and caused the levees to break.

Water Everywhere

Patrick LeBau looked out his window. Below him, deep water rushed down the street. He thought Hurricane Katrina had already gone. The rain had stopped, and the 150-mile-per-hour winds had already died down. "Where is all this water coming from?" he wondered.

He never dreamed that the **levees** had burst. Levees are high walls that were built throughout the city. They were supposed to protect the city from flooding.

Patrick stayed at the window with family members and friends. They were curious at first. The water was not stopping. It was getting deeper. Soon, Patrick's house began to flood. The water was rising fast. He left the valuable antique gun collection that had belonged to his grandfather.

He barely had enough time to grab a few clothes and get out of there.

Patrick and his family had decided not to **evacuate** when they heard a Category Five hurricane named Katrina was barreling straight toward New Orleans. Category Five is the strongest a hurricane can be. Usually at that strength, a storm is deadly. Hurricane Katrina, however, had seemed to cause fairly little damage in New Orleans.

SAFFIR-SIMPSON SCALE

CATEGORY	WINDS (MPH)	SURGE (feet)
	74-95	4-5
	96-110	6-8
	111-130	9-12
	131-155	13-18
	>155	>18

Weather experts use the **Saffir-Simpson scale** to describe a storm's strength. Higher wind speeds bring more water, resulting in a **storm surge**.

New Orleans is one of the few major cities in the world to lie below sea level. It is a vital **port** city for the United States because it is located at the mouth of the Mississippi River. **Engineers** figured out how to surround the area with levees and pump the water out. The city was built, and many people moved in—but if the levees broke, there was risk of deadly floods.

It wasn't until a few hours after Hurricane Katrina struck that the water started pouring through or over several levees. Water was spilling everywhere. The whole city of New Orleans was in danger of being under water.

Patrick and his family and friends fled their homes and trudged through the rushing water to the Superdome, a football stadium for the New Orleans Saints. A hurricane shelter had been set up there.

Patrick and his friends found the Superdome to be an unsafe place. It was overcrowded, and there was no power. The air inside was hot and thick. People were running out of food and water. There were reports of crime, and there were not enough police or security officers to maintain order.

An aerial shot of one of New Orleans' broken levees shows just how much water was pouring into the city streets after the hurricane made landfall.

City residents who did not evacuate the city thought they would be safe inside the Superdome. They quickly ran out of food and water, and conditions got worse when the power went out.

Patrick is an American soldier who had just returned home to New Orleans from fighting a war in Iraq (eye-RAK). He said he was shocked by some of the violence he saw in his home city. He knew that in order to keep his family and friends safe, they would have to get out of New Orleans.

But where would they go? And what was happening to his city?

A picture of Hurricane Katrina—a Category 5 storm—was taken by a satellite in space. The hurricane was so huge, it covered the entire state of Florida and much of the Gulf of Mexico.

Escape from New Orleans

The United States is lucky to have the National Hurricane Center, an agency that tracks hurricanes. Some countries don't know a hurricane is coming until it hits them. Normally the National Hurricane Center is able to track storms a few weeks before they make **landfall** near the United States. Hurricane Katrina was different right from the start. It seemed to hit New Orleans and the rest of the Gulf Coast area by surprise.

In the early morning hours of August 23, the hurricane center discovered a fierce weather pattern forming very quickly just south of the Bahamas—islands that lie south and east of Florida and New Orleans. Two days later, the storm was named Hurricane Katrina. Even though it had missed Florida's mainland, it still swatted the southernmost tip—the Florida Keys. It killed 11 people there.

The people and governments of Louisiana, Mississippi, and Alabama began to take notice that this killer storm might just be headed their way. They started to prepare. They ordered evacuations of many areas, including New Orleans. Many people, like Patrick LeBau, thought they were safer and better off just waiting out the storm in their homes.

Believe it or not, New Orleans was lucky. On August 29, six days after it was detected in the Bahamas, Katrina made landfall about 70 miles east of New Orleans. It slammed into Buras, Louisiana, and Gulfport, Mississippi.

In New Orleans, heavy rain and strong winds whipped through the city. Hundreds of trees fell, and there was other damage, but the city had been spared . . . or had it? The city's real problems started after the hurricane had passed. When the levees failed and the water pumps stopped working, the real nightmare began.

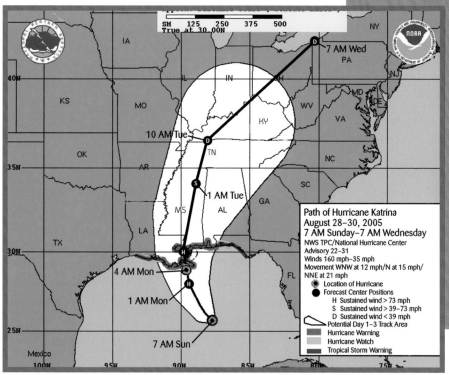

As Katrina approached the Louisiana and Mississippi coast, the National Hurricane Center drew maps showing where the hurricane would probably go. The scientists were right in their predictions. The storm ripped through Louisiana, Mississippi, and Alabama before losing power inland.

People who had stayed in the city were no longer safe in their homes. The shelters—mainly the New Orleans Superdome and the Ernest N. Morial Convention Center—weren't safe, either.

There was only one thing left to do, and that was escape.

People who did not evacuate or find refuge in the Superdome climbed up onto their roofs and waved to passing helicopters for help. Many were stranded up there for days because their homes and the streets were flooded.

CHAPTER THREE

Where Is the Help?

Everyone was ordered to leave the city. Some people were stranded on their rooftops, and some were still in hospitals. Thousands were without food or water. Rescue and relief workers were desperately needed. Kathleen Blanco, the governor of Louisiana, had issued a state of emergency. This **declaration** allowed her to ask for help from troops in the National Guard. Many of those troops were serving overseas as the United States continued its war with Iraq. There were fewer soldiers than the governor wanted.

Other states promised to help. They would send soldiers, relief workers, and other forms of aid. Even other countries were offering help. Large countries like Australia and England and small countries like Cuba and Sri Lanka offered to send money, soldiers, or whatever else the United States needed.

The Federal Emergency Management Agency (FEMA) also promised a quick and strong response to the emergency. However, a few days after the hurricane had passed, there was still very little help coming in.

The officials at FEMA continued to promise help and asked for patience. After all, they argued, it takes time to **mobilize** help and send people to the right places. Critics pointed out that the United States is very quick when it comes to helping other countries. It was hard to understand why the country was so slow to help its own citizens.

People were getting angry. They wanted to leave New Orleans. There was word that armed bandits had taken over the city. People started breaking into stores by smashing windows. They walked away with whatever goods they could carry.

Strong winds had ripped off part of the roof of the Superdome, and water was seeping in. Toilets were no longer working. The thousands of people who had found shelter there needed to get out.

Looters took advantage of the disaster. They broke into stores and homes to steal whatever they could. The Army National Guard was sent in to stop the thievery.

The water that had filled the city's streets began to go down. People started leaving the Superdome and other shelters. Patrick LeBau and his family headed toward Baton Rouge, 80 miles away. Others did, too. Still others took buses to Florida or Texas.

"We have relatives in Texas," said Gloria Peters, who had left the Superdome with 14 family members and friends. "We're going to try and make it to them and stay with them. I mean, we have nothing left. We have nothing."

Water from the broken levees swamped the city and turned the streets into rivers. The muddy water was extremely dangerous. It was filled with germs. Strong currents could wash away cars and even mobile homes.

Heroes Arrive

News reporters began to talk about the government's slow response to the tragedy. Pictures of dead bodies floating in the streets were shown on the nightly news. Americans began to respond with help.

Heroes took many different forms. Some of them were schoolchildren who collected money to pay for supplies such as food, water, and clothing. Their parents held bake sales to raise money. Volunteer firefighters, who normally use Labor Day weekend to raise money for their own operations, sent whatever they raised to relief **organizations**. Police forces sent truckloads of socks, shoes, and blankets to the police officers in New Orleans who had been working day and night since the storm hit and the levees broke.

Tired of poor conditions inside the Superdome and the Convention Center, city of New Orleans residents gathered on raised highways. They observed the damage and waited to be rescued.

Army trucks arrived with much-needed supplies. When soldiers made it to the Convention Center, many of the people cheered. Some people asked what had taken so long.

During this time, stories of individual heroism were being told. Some of those stories included famous entertainers like actor Sean Penn and singer Harry Connick Jr. They took boats out

Two men try to paddle their way around the flooded New Orleans streets. It would be weeks before the water receded and the levees were repaired.

onto the water and rescued people who were stranded in their homes. Connick took the shirt off his back to put around an old man who had been trapped in his house for days.

Other heroes included four women **paramedics** from Hawaii who had traveled to New Orleans for a work-related meeting. They carried injured hotel guests to safety, tended to sick

U.S. Army Captain Jesse Stewart surveys the debris left behind at the Superdome. The army played a pivotal role in the rescue of thousands of people from the disaster site.

people at the shelters, and then treated police officers for **exhaustion** and **dehydration**. The four women were greeted as heroes when they returned home to Hawaii.

Another person who went above and beyond what his job asked of him was Army Chief Warrant Officer Dan Culberson. He spent five straight days flying a Chinook helicopter trying to save lives. He stopped only to eat quick meals and

An Army guardsman is sprayed with a decontaminating agent. It will kill any **bacteria** or other germs he may have picked up from the floodwaters.

to refuel his helicopter. On each trip, he could take only 30 people. He made so many trips, he saved an incredible 839 lives.

There would be many more heroic tales in the weeks and months to come. Most would never get reported on the news, but they were still appreciated.

Chinook helicopters were used to drop sandbags into the holes in the levees. The sandbags would help keep more water from flooding the city of New Orleans.

New Orleans Rises Again

For rescue workers, the main goal was to rescue people who had been stranded in their homes and to evacuate those who were in other dangerous places. The engineers would figure out how to repair the broken levees.

To stop the water that was still flooding into the city, workers filled thousands and thousands of bags with sand. Helicopters placed the 300-pound sandbags into the holes in the levees. Once that was done, engineers could reach the city's pumps, repair them, and start drying the streets.

Repairing the levees and drying the streets took several days. Before these tasks were finished, hundreds of city residents had died.

CHAPTER FIVE

Some had drowned, some had died of dehydration, and others had starved to death.

"How many people died as a result of us not having the resources to get people water, to get them pulled out of harm's way quick enough to get them evacuated out of the city?" asked New Orleans Mayor Ray Nagin.

The full scope of damage caused by Hurricane Katrina will not be known for years. According to some reports, at least 1,200 people died in New Orleans and in neighboring Alabama and Mississippi. The storm caused $130 billion in damage. Because most of the homes in New Orleans had been made out of wood, many would have to be knocked down and rebuilt. Others would have lasting water damage and mold problems. Colleges, schools, and businesses would also be closed for a long time.

The federal government took a lot of blame for slow relief and rescue efforts. However, President George W. Bush promised the country that the city of New Orleans, also called the Crescent City, would be rebuilt even better than it once was.

A tractor begins to clean away debris. The cleanup effort was an overwhelming task. Many people volunteered to help, but there was a shortage of dump trucks and other equipment for them to use.

"These days of sorrow and outrage have also been marked by acts of courage and kindness that make all Americans proud," he said. "We will do what it takes, we will stay as long as it takes, to help citizens rebuild their communities and their lives. And all who question the future of the Crescent City need to know there is no way to imagine America without New Orleans, and this great city will rise again."

CHRONOLOGY

August 23, 2005	National Hurricane Center recognizes a weather disturbance that will become Hurricane Katrina.
August 27	Katrina becomes a "major hurricane."
August 28	The Superdome opens for evacuees. Mayor Ray Nagin orders people to evacuate New Orleans; not everyone leaves.
August 29	6:00 A.M. Hurricane Katrina makes landfall in Buras, Louisiana, 70 miles from New Orleans. 8:00 A.M. Levees begin to fail. 9:00 A.M. Parts of Superdome roof are torn off. People begin breaking into stores and stealing whatever they can carry.
August 30	Louisiana National Guardsmen are deployed. Search and rescue operations continue, with 350 boats in the water and two groups of helicopters flying overhead. Ernest N. Morial Convention Center is open for evacuees, but it is not stocked with food and water. By the end of the day, 80 percent of the city is under water.
August 31	More National Guardsmen are deployed. Governor Blanco calls for total evacuation of the city. Superdome evacuation begins, and people are bused to Houston, Texas.
September 1	More National Guardsmen are deployed; rescue helicopters try to evacuate the Superdome.
September 2	President Bush visits New Orleans.
September 5	A forced evacuation of the city is under way.
September 15	President Bush promises that New Orleans will be rebuilt and rise again.
August 2006	New Orleans schools begin reopening on the one year anniversary of Katrina.

FIND OUT MORE

Books

Editors of Time Magazine. *Time: Hurricane Katrina: The Storm That Changed America.* Alexandria, Virginia: Time, 2005.

Moyer, Susan M. *Hurricane Katrina: Stories of Rescue, Recovery and Rebuilding in the Eye of the Storm.* Champaign, Illinois: Spotlight Press LLC, 2005.

Vidrine, T. L. *Suffering Katrina: Personal Stories From Hurricane Katrina's Survivors.* Charleston, South Carolina: BookSurge Publishing, 2005.

On the Internet

FEMA for Kids
http://www.fema.gov/kids/
Hurricane Katrina Photo Gallery
http://www.katrina.com/hurricanekatrina/photos/photogallery/
photogallery.com
National Weather Service
http://www.nws.noaa.gov/
National Hurricane Center
http://www.nhc.noaa.gov/

Works Consulted

This book is based on the author's personal trip to Louisiana in September 2005, immediately after Hurricane Katrina ravaged the Gulf Coast. The author interviewed dozens of survivors from New Orleans and witnessed the destruction firsthand. His interviews covered people in New Orleans and evacuees in Baton Rouge, including the following:

Personal interview with Gloria Peters at Louisiana State University in Baton Rouge, September 2, 2005.

Personal interview with Patrick LeBau at Louisiana State University in Baton Rouge, September 2, 2005.

Personal interview with Ronald Evans at Baton Rouge Riverside Center, September 3, 2005.

Associated Press, September 1, 2005; as reported by Josh White and Peter Whoriskey in "Planning, Response Are Faulted," *Washington Post,* Friday, September 2, 2005, p. A01.

CNN.com, "Levee Plan Prompts Call to 'Come Home,'" December 15, 2005, http://www.cnn.com/2005/POLITICS/12/15/bush.levees/?section=cnn_space

CNN.com, "Military Due to Move In to New Orleans," September 2, 2005.

CNN.com, "World Leaders Offer Sympathy, Aid," September 2, 2005.

Davis, Sandy, and Jessica Fender. "Evacuees Recount Ordeal Waiting for Help to Arrive," *The Advocate,* September 3, 2005, p. 10A.

Farhad Manjoo, Page Rockwell, and Aaron Kinney. "Timeline to Disaster." Salon.com, September 15, 2005, http://www.salon.com/news/feature/2005/09/15/katrina_timeline/index_np.html

Gannett News Service Special Report: "Katrina Heroes."

Goldberg, Michelle. "Homeless Again in New Orleans." Salon.com, February 7, 2006, http://www.salon.com/news/feature/2006/02/07/hotels/index_np.html

Knight Ridder, Washington Bureau, "Government's Failures Doomed Many in Katrina's Path," September 11, 2005.

Ortega, Juan. "Local Unit Will Assist in Rescue," *Florida Today,* August 31, 2005, p. 7A.

Schweid, Barry, AP Diplomatic Writer. "Aid Pours In from Around Globe," *The Advocate,* September 3, 2005, p. 10A.

Today show with Katie Couric, September 6, 2005.

"Transcript: Bush Katrina Address," September 15, 2005, http://www.foxnews.com/story/0,2933,169514,00.html

VandeHei, Jim, and Peter Baker. "Bush Pledges Historic Effort To Help Gulf Coast Recover; President Says U.S. Will Learn From Mistakes," *Washington Post,* September 16, 2005, p. A01.

GLOSSARY

bacteria (bak-TEE-ree-ah)—Microorganisms of various forms that often cause sickness and disease.

declaration (deh-cluh-RAY-shun)—A major announcement or promise.

dehydration (dee-hy-DRAY-shun)—An unhealthy drying out of the body from lack of drinking water.

engineers (en-jeh-NEERS)—People who figure out how to do construction projects.

exhaustion (ek-ZAWS-chun)—The state of being completely and extremely tired.

evacuate (ee-VAA-kyoo-ayt)—To leave a dangerous place.

landfall—Reaching land, usually from the sea.

levee (LEH-vee)—A built-up embankment meant to keep a body of water from overflowing.

mobilize (MOH-bih-lyz)—To assemble and make ready for action.

organization (or-gah-nih-ZAY-shun)—A group or society whose members have a common goal.

paramedic (pahr-uh-MEH-dik)—A specially trained person who provides emergency medical treatment.

port—An area with a harbor for loading and unloading goods.

Saffir-Simpson Scale (SAA-feer SIMP-son)—A 1 to 5 rating system for measuring hurricane intensity.

storm surge (STORM surj)—An extra high water level caused when a storm pushes seawater ashore while dumping rain from above.

INDEX